MOSES
IN THE BULRUSHES

RETOLD AND ILLUSTRATED BY WARWICK HUTTON

A MARGARET K. MC ELDERRY BOOK

ATHENEUM   1986   NEW YORK

This book is for Pete & Anne

Library of Congress Catalog Card Number: 85-72261
ISBN 0-689-50393-8
Copyright © 1986 by Warwick Hutton
All rights reserved
Published simultaneously in Canada by Collier Macmillan Canada, Inc.
Manufactured by Dai Nippon Printing Company in Japan
First edition

The Pharoah, king of Egypt, was alarmed. "Behold the people of Israel are more numerous and mightier than we are," he said. To reduce their numbers, he decreed that all boy babies born to Hebrew women must be killed.

There was a Hebrew family called Levi,

and when a son was born to them

the mother, seeing that he was a healthy child,

decided to hide him carefully for three months, hoping to save his life.

When she could no longer conceal him, she made a little ark of bulrushes and daubed it with mud and pitch.

She put her baby in it and hid the ark among the flags
and rushes by the river's edge.

The baby's sister stood a little way off to see what would happen to the baby.

Now the daughter of the king came down to bathe in the river, while her maidens walked along the riverbank.

The Pharoah's daughter saw the ark and sent a maid to fetch it.

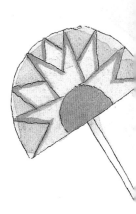

When she opened it, she found a baby inside. The baby
began to cry.

The Pharoah's daughter took pity on him.

"This must be one of the Hebrew children," she said. The baby's sister came near to the Pharoah's daughter. "Shall I find a nurse among the Hebrew women for you," she asked, "so the baby can be cared for?"

The Pharoah's daughter asked her to do so. The girl went and called her—and the baby's—own mother.

When she came, the Pharoah's daughter said, "Take this
child and nurse it for me, and I will pay you wages."
And the mother did so gladly.

The child grew, and when he was older, his mother brought him back to the Pharoah's daughter, and she adopted him as her son.

"I will call him Moses," she said.

And when Moses grew to be a man and saw how the
Hebrews were persecuted, he led the children of Israel
out of Egypt to the Promised Land, as the Lord had
commanded him. Moses was a man of God and lived
to be a hundred and twenty years old.

THE END